CONCORD
CONCORD BRANCH LIBRARY
2900 SALVIO STREET
CONCORD, CALIFORNIA 94519
JAN 02 2007
D0016568

roxie
and the hooligans

roxie and

the hooligans

BY PHYLLIS REYNOLDS NAYLOR

WITH ILLUSTRATIONS BY ALEXANDRA BOIGER

CONTRA COSTA COUNTY LIBRARY

WITHDRAWN

ginee seo books

ATHENEUM BOOKS FOR YOUNG READERS

NEW YORK LONDON TORONTO SYDNEY

3 1901 03733 8979

Atheneum Books for Young Readers
An imprint of Simon & Schuster Children's
Publishing Division
1230 Avenue of the Americas
New York, New York 10020
This book is a work of fiction. Any references to historical events, real people, or real locales are used fictitiously. Other names, characters, places, and incidents are products of the author's imagination, and any resemblance to actual events or locales or persons, living or dead, is entirely coincidental.
Text copyright © 2006 by Phyllis Reynolds Naylor
Illustrations copyright © 2006 by Alexandra Boiger
All rights reserved, including the right of reproduction in whole or in part in any form.
Book design by Ann Bobco
The text for this book is set in Augustal.
The illustrations for this book are rendered in pencil.
Manufactured in the United States of America
First Edition
10 9 8 7 6 5 4 3 2 1
Library of Congress Cataloging-in-Publication Data
Naylor, Phyllis Reynolds.
Roxie and the Hooligans / Phyllis Reynolds Naylor ;
illustrated by Alexandra Boiger.—1st ed.
p. cm.
"Ginee Seo Books."
Summary: Roxie Warbler, the niece of a famous explorer, follows Uncle Dangerfoot's advice on how to survive any crisis when she becomes stranded on an island with a gang of school bullies and a pair of murderous bank robbers.
ISBN-13: 978-1-4169-0243-0
ISBN-10: 1-4169-0243-0
[1. Adventure and adventurers—
Fiction. 2. Resourcefulness—Fiction.
3. Survival—Fiction. 4. Bullies—Fiction.]
I. Boiger, Alexandra, ill. II. Title.
PZ7.N24Do 2006
[Fic]—dc22 2004024645

To Garrett Riley Naylor, the newest member of our family,
with love
—P. R. N.

To Andrea, with love. And to Vanessa, who brought
all the little Roxies to life.
—A. B.

Books by Phyllis Reynolds Naylor

The Witch Books

Witch's Sister
Witch Water
The Witch Herself
The Witch's Eye
Witch Weed
The Witch Returns

Picture Books

The Boy with the Helium Head
Old Sadie and the Christmas Bear
Keeping a Christmas Secret
King of the Playground
Ducks Disappearing
I Can't Take You Anywhere
Sweet Strawberries
Please DO Feed the Bears

Books for Young Readers

How Lazy Can You Get?
All Because I'm Older
Maudie in the Middle
One of the Third-Grade Thonkers
Josie's Troubles

Books for Middle Readers

Walking Through the Dark
How I Came to Be a Writer
Eddie, Incorporated
The Solomon System
The Keeper
Beetles, Lightly Toasted
The Fear Place
Being Danny's Dog
Danny's Desert Rats
Walker's Crossing

Books for Older Readers

A String of Chances
Night Cry
The Dark of the Tunnel
The Year of the Gopher
Send No Blessings
Ice
Sang Spell
Jade Green
Blizzard's Wake

Shiloh Books

Shiloh

Shiloh Season

Saving Shiloh

The Alice Books

Starting with Alice

Alice in Blunderland

Lovingly Alice

The Agony of Alice

Alice in Rapture, Sort of

Reluctantly Alice

All But Alice

Alice in April

Alice In-Between

Alice the Brave

Alice in Lace

Outrageously Alice

Achingly Alice

Alice on the Outside

The Grooming of Alice

Alice Alone

Simply Alice

Patiently Alice

Including Alice

Alice on Her Way

The Bernie Magruder Books

Bernie Magruder and the Case of the Big Stink

Bernie Magruder and the Disappearing Bodies

Bernie Magruder and the Haunted Hotel

Bernie Magruder and the Drive-thru Funeral Parlor

Bernie Magruder and the Bus Station Blowup

Bernie Magruder and the Pirate's Treasure

Bernie Magruder and the Parachute Peril

Bernie Magruder and the Bats in the Belfry

The Cat Pack Mysteries

The Grand Escape

The Healing of Texas Jake

Carlotta's Kittens

Polo's Mother

The York Trilogy

Shadows on the Wall

Faces in the Water

Footprints at the Window

contents

• UNCLE DANGERFOOT •

When Uncle Dangerfoot came to visit, everything in the house had to be just so.

The footstool was arranged in its place, the tea piping hot, the crumpets and jam on a platter, and Roxie Warbler watched for him at the door. The man who had wrestled alligators and jumped from planes was not to be kept waiting.

"And there he is!" cried Mrs. Warbler as her brother stepped handsomely out of a cab and came briskly up the walk. He wore a jungle helmet, a tan safari jacket with brass buttons, and he carried a long slender cane, which could, in an instant, become a harpoon, a gun, an umbrella, or a walking stick, depending on the circumstances and the weather.

Nine-year-old Roxie looked forward to his visits, for he had traveled all over the world with Lord Thistlebottom from London. And Thistlebottom was famous for his book, *Lord Thistlebottom's Book of Pitfalls and How to Survive Them.*

"Hello, Uncle Dangerfoot!" Roxie called, throwing open the door as he came up the steps.

The man with the handlebar mustache smiled down at his niece and tapped her fondly on the head with his walking stick. And that was about all the attention Roxie would get from her uncle, for although she had put on her best blue dress and her patent-leather shoes and she had brushed her hair till her scalp tingled, Uncle Dangerfoot was not a man of emotion and never hugged anyone if he could help it.

"Come in! Come in!" said Roxie's father, shaking Uncle Dangerfoot's hand and ushering him to the big easy chair with the footstool at the ready. "We are so glad to have you."

"So eager to hear about your latest adventure!" said Roxie's mother.

Roxie just stood to one side beaming, holding the platter of crumpets until her uncle noticed and helped himself. Then she sat down on the floor at his feet, waiting to leap to attention

should he need some extra cream for his tea or a second lump of sugar.

"Oh, it was harrowing, let me tell you!" said Uncle Dangerfoot, taking a small sip of tea, then biting into his crumpet and jam. "It was uncharted territory in Australia, and our canteens had long since run dry. . . ."

Roxie hung on every word, even though her uncle's stories tended to go on all evening. The crumpets and tea would be gone, and her uncle would still be talking. The flames in the fireplace would have died down and gone out, and he would still be talking. Sometimes Roxie was embarrassed by drifting off to sleep in spite of herself, and her father would carry her upstairs and tuck her in bed. But parts of her uncle's stories always lingered in her head:

". . . So there we were, our lips parched, our mouths full of dust, our throats so dry we could scarcely speak. 'Do not panic!' Lord Thistlebottom said to me as we followed the dry streambed. 'Look for a sharp bend in the bed and keep an eye out for wet sand.' I, of course, having the sharper eye, spied it shortly, and there we dug down, down, down until we found seeping water. . . ."

"I'm thirsty," Roxie murmured, her own lips feeling parched, her throat dry. She opened her eyes to find that, once again, she was back in her bed, a glass of water on the night table, the first faint glow of morning coming through her window shade, and Uncle Dangerfoot, of course, gone.

She drank a little of the water and pulled the covers up under her chin. If only she could be as brave as her uncle. What a disappointment she must be! Not only did she sometimes fall asleep during his visits, but while he was afraid of nothing, Roxie Warbler was afraid of a lot of things: thunder, lightning, tornadoes, floods, and, most of all, Public School Number Thirty-Seven, where Helvetia's Hooligans seemed to have chosen Roxie to be their Victim of the Year.

It was her ears, of course. They were round ears, pink ears, ears of the normal variety, and Roxie scrubbed them daily inside and behind. But they stuck straight out from her head like the handles on a sugar bowl, the ears on an elephant, the wings on a bat.

And though Roxie Warbler was neither fat nor thin, short nor tall, pretty nor plain, smart nor stupid—a perfectly average child in the fourth grade at Public School Number Thirty-

Seven—her ears were the first thing anyone noticed when they looked at her and the only thing they seemed to remember.

From that first day of school a month ago, when Roxie started up the walk to the building, Helvetia Hagus had watched her come, and her eyes narrowed. So did the eyes of her little band of hooligans: Simon Surly, Freddy Filch, and the smallest, leanest, meanest hooligan of them all—a wiry little hornet of a girl called Smoky Jo.

When Roxie had got up close to them, it was Smoky Jo who squealed, "Why, Grandma, what big ears you have!" and the other hooligans laughed and hooted.

Helvetia brayed like a donkey: "*Hee*-yah, *hee*-yah!"

Simon howled like a hyena: "Hoo-hoo ha-ha, hoo-hoo ha-ha!"

Freddy cawed like a crow: "Ca-*haw*! Ca-*haw*!"

And Smoky Jo squeaked like a mouse: "*Eeek*a. *Eeek*a. *Eeek*a."

Together, their braying and howling and cawing and squeaking sounded to Roxie like feeding time at the circus—and trouble for Roxie Warbler. Roxie had tried her best to smile and be friendly, but that only made the teasing worse.

"I think we ought to tape those ears to the sides of her head where they belong," said Helvetia Hagus, a large-boned girl with a square face and a square frame who wore her kneesocks rolled down around her ankles.

"I think we ought to find something to *hang*

on those ears," said Simon Surly, who was as tall and skinny as a broom. When he was feeling nasty, his lips curled down on the left side and up on the right.

"I think we ought to find something to *pour* in those ears," said Freddy Filch, a round, red-faced boy who wheezed when he talked.

Smoky Jo had eyes that positively gleamed, and her short hair circled her head like a barbed-wire fence. "*I* think we should hang *her* up by the ears!" she squealed, and they brayed and howled and cawed and squeaked some more.

Every day it happened again, only each day the hooligans crowded a little closer around Roxie. It did not happen in the classroom, where the teacher, Miss Crumbly, could see. And Roxie did not want to bother her parents about it, for how could the niece of the man who braved sandstorms and avalanches tell her parents that she was afraid of a small band of hooligans on the playground?

She had almost memorized Lord Thistlebottom's book by heart. Every bit of advice was followed by the admonition *Do not panic.* Roxie knew that if she were ever lost in the desert, she should try to sit at least twelve inches off the ground, because the ground could be thirty degrees hotter than the air. *Do not panic.*

She knew that if you are jumping from a plane and your parachute does not open, head for water if you can. *Do not panic.*

Roxie knew that if she found herself on top of a moving train, she should not try to stand up. *Do not panic.*

But she did not know what to do about Helvetia's Hooligans, who had chosen Roxie Warbler to tease and torment and otherwise make miserable for every day of her life in Public School Number Thirty-Seven.

• HELVETIA'S HOOLIGANS •

Of course, not all children on this little-known stretch of New England's shoreline behaved so abominably. Farther up the coast in the town of Hasty Pudding, children were especially kind. In the town below that, in Hamburger-on-Bun, children were well mannered, and even the boys and girls of Swiss-on-Rye were known to be friendly.

By the time you got down as far as Chin-in-Hand, however, where Mr. and Mrs. Warbler had moved with their daughter, people just didn't much care. Times were hard, and there were other things to worry about.

So every morning Roxie got out of bed and put on her school uniform—her green kneesocks, her brown and green plaid skirt, her green shirt and brown jacket. Her clothes were about as dull as she felt inside.

She bravely said good-bye to her father and kissed her mother and wondered how to get through another day. If she went early, she discovered, she could go inside and help the teacher dust the erasers. But then the hooligans waited for her *after* school and tried to hang their book bags on her ears.

So she asked the teacher if she could stay in after school as well and empty wastebaskets. Miss Crumbly said, "Of course!"

But when Roxie came out, the hooligans were still there, and they tried to tape her ears to the sides of her head with strapping tape. Her hair stuck to the tape and her ears burned, and when she finally got away and ran home, she had red marks on both cheeks.

The only person who befriended her was a large boy named Norman, who wore thick glasses and had to squint to read his primer.

"Those kids are like sharks, Roxie," he said. "They're mean to me, too. They're always trying to take my glasses. Then I can't see anything at all, and I bump into stuff."

"I know," said Roxie.

"I'd help if I could," said Norman.

"I know," said Roxie.

If only she was *half* as brave as Uncle Dangerfoot. If only she was *one fourth* as brave as Lord Thistlebottom. If only he would write *The Book of Hooligans and How to Survive Them.*

Roxie told her mother that she would be going to school very, *very* early each morning to help her teacher. And she would be staying very, *very* late to help even more.

"Just how many erasers can you possibly dust?" asked Mrs. Warbler.

"How many wastebaskets can you empty? How many desks are there to wipe?" asked Mr. Warbler.

"Oh, there's a lot of work to be done," said Roxie. And her parents were glad to know that she was a help to the teacher, so they let her be.

One Tuesday, Roxie got up an hour early. She made her own toast and cocoa and got to school just as the sun was beginning to rise over the ocean a block away. The only other person at school at this hour was Norman, sitting on a bench and eating a breakfast of fish-and-chips. Not even the teachers or principal had come to school yet, so Roxie and Norman sat together and watched the gulls circling over the playground.

And then Roxie saw them—the hooligans—coming through the gate. Freddy Filch was holding something gray under one arm, and Smoky Jo was waving something white in the air.

"What have they got?" Norman asked, squinting his eyes.

"I don't know. Smoky Jo looks like she's carrying a flag, maybe," said Roxie. And she began to hope. A truce flag, perhaps? A peace flag?

The hooligans were yelling.

"What are they saying?" asked Norman.

"I'm not sure," said Roxie.

The hooligans came straight toward them. Smoky Jo was not waving a flag at all. She was waving a pair of her brother's underpants, and Freddy, strangely, was carrying a carton of eggs.

"Hey, Roxie!" said Helvetia. "We figured your head was cold."

"Yeah, Roxie. You need a cap!" said Simon Surly.

"Your ears will just fit through the leg holes," said Smoky Jo, swinging the underpants around and around over her head like a lasso.

"And *then,*" said Freddy Filch, "we're going to glue those pants to your head with eggs. You'll be the Slimy Creature from Public School Number Thirty-Seven."

"Run, Roxie!" whispered Norman.

"What'd you say, old boy?" asked Simon, snatching his glasses.

"Give those back!" Norman demanded, but he couldn't even see who had them.

Roxie leaped off the bench and began to run, but the hooligans had blocked the gate. All she could do was run around and around the playground. The hooligans picked up gravel and threw it at her legs to make her stop.

Roxie's heart was racing. Her head began to pound. *Do not panic,* she remembered. *To avoid gunfire, run in a zigzag line.* Roxie ran in a zigzag line. *Ping* went a piece of gravel as it hit the school building. *Pong* went another piece as it hit a swing.

There must be something I can do! Roxie thought in desperation. *There must be somewhere I can hide!* If only she could get inside the building . . . But she tried the door and it was locked. Then she saw that a window was open ten feet off the ground. The school's big blue Dumpster sat beneath the window. Two trash cans sat beside the Dumpster.

Roxie made a dash toward that corner of the building. *Splat!* Something hit her ankle. Freddy was throwing eggs.

Roxie scrambled on top of one of the trash cans. *Splog!* Another egg hit her knee and began

sliding down her leg as Roxie climbed up the side of the Dumpster.

"She's going for the open window!" shouted Helvetia as more eggs hit Roxie or landed on the rim of the Dumpster. "After her!"

There came the sound of scraping and scrambling as the hooligans began to climb. Freddy must have decided to throw all the eggs now, Roxie realized, to keep her from reaching the window, for they splattered here and there.

At the top Roxie shakily got to her feet and tried to balance as she started along the Dumpster's rim toward the window. Raw eggs hit her knees. They covered her shoes. They glistened on the rim of the Dumpster. Roxie held her arms straight out at her sides as though she were Uncle Dangerfoot crossing a river on a log, but the eggs made it too slippery, and just before Smoky Jo's head appeared over the edge of the Dumpster, Roxie fell in.

It was warm and wet and smelly in the Dumpster. It smelled like banana peel, paste pots, and old gym suits, but Roxie didn't make a sound.

"Hey!" yelled Smoky Jo. "She's not here! I don't see her!"

"Then old Elephant Ears must have got through that window!" bellowed Helvetia as she too came over the top, then Freddy and Simon, all struggling to raise themselves up and walk along the Dumpster's rim to the open window of the school.

But one by one, they slipped on the slimy eggs and fell in—Helvetia up to her armpits,

Simon up to his chin, Freddy with only his nose sticking out, and Smoky Jo upside down.

Just at that moment Roxie heard a terrible roar from outside, like a dragon with a bellyache. Above the roar she heard Norman's frantic yell.

And before she could get one leg out of the garbage, before she could even peek out over the bin, the roar became deafening. She heard a *clank,* then a *clunk,* and in the next instant Roxie and the hooligans were tumbling about inside the Dumpster as it rose up, up into the air. Little did they know that it had been lifted onto the back of a flatbed truck, and soon they would be rolling down the highway toward the sea.

• INTO THE SEA •

If you are buried *in an avalanche, do not panic. Dig a hole around you and spit. The saliva will fall downward, telling you which direction is up.*

Roxie knew that Lord Thistlebottom and Uncle Dangerfoot had been buried in snow once, but she bet they had never been buried in garbage. Either way, snow or garbage, it was dark where she was. How was she supposed to see which way her saliva was falling?

Roxie spit. It landed back on her face. She began clawing at the garbage above her only to find, when she reached the top, that Helvetia Hagus had got there first.

"I'll get you for this!" Helvetia spluttered, a banana peel draped over her head.

Another head appeared, attached to Simon Surly. Then a hand belonging to Freddy Filch popped up and a foot that could only be Smoky Jo's.

"We'll get you, Roxie Warbler!" they all cried, struggling to grab her through the glop.

But who could know that the truck had reached the water's edge? Suddenly the Dumpster began to tip. Roxie and the hooligans began to slide. When they could hold on no longer, out they spilled along with the garbage onto a barge that soon left shore. And there they were, on their way out to sea.

The barge had an acre of garbage on it, from dozens and dozens of Dumpsters, and though it was open at the top so that Roxie could see the sky, the sides were steep and slippery with the stinky mix of rotten sausage and spoiled fruit. Whenever the hooligans emerged from the stuff, a hand bobbing up here, a leg over there, they looked like slimy sausages themselves, their hair plastered to their heads with hamburger grease.

"We'll get you, Roxie Warbler!" they bellowed, spitting out bits of moldy cheese and fish scales.

"We'll throttle your engine!" cried Simon Surly.

"We'll blow your whistle!" yelled Freddy Filch.

"We'll stop your clock!" screeched Smoky Jo.

On and on the barge went, farther and farther out into the ocean, as Roxie and the hooligans tried to stay on top of the mess.

Just when they had her surrounded, the tugboat pushing the barge slowed to a stop. The hinges on the barge began to creak, the bottom opened, and suddenly Roxie Warbler and Helvetia's Hooligans went sliding, sliding, sliding down into the water. The last noise they heard was the sucking sound of the sea as it swallowed the load of grapefruit rinds and coffee grounds, old gym suits and paste pots. And then five filthy children began swimming for their lives.

Now, all the students of Public School Number Thirty-Seven knew how to swim because they lived so near the ocean. Every year on the first day of first grade, every child was taken to the local pool to learn to stay afloat. Every year on the last day of first grade, every child was taken to the pool once again and thrown into the water. If he hadn't learned to swim before, he learned now.

So it was no accident that the five children all rose to the surface, blubbering and blowing. As the tugboat and barge grew smaller and smaller in the distance, heading back to shore, the five children looked about them to see just what kind of a fix they were in.

You would think that the four hooligans, having almost been buried alive in a Dumpster and drowned at sea, would forget about chasing someone with big ears. You would think they might want to work together to get back to their parents in Chin-in-Hand.

But Helvetia's Hooligans just seemed angrier

than ever at Roxie Warbler. If she had only stood still on the playground, they seemed to be thinking, and had let them put the underpants on her head, with her ears sticking out the leg holes and slimy eggs plastering it to her skull, none of this would have happened.

And so, when Roxie spied an island not far off, she began swimming as fast as she could, and the hooligans followed—foreheads furrowed, faces grim, and with every stroke of their hooligan arms, they muttered, "Get Roxie. . . . Get Roxie. . . . Get Roxie. . . ."

Roxie swam faster than anyone, if only because she was the most frightened. She plunged forward as soon as she felt land beneath her feet and—gasping and panting—splashed out of the water, her wet clothes clinging to her skin. But it was too late. Simon Surly was the second-fastest swimmer, and he too reached the shore. Slithering along on his belly, he grabbed her ankle, bringing her down on the sand.

When attacked by an alligator, Lord Thistlebottom had written, *do not panic. Cover the beast's eyes and try to climb on its back.*

Over and over they tumbled, but Roxie covered Simon's eyes with her hands and climbed onto his back. Simon could not see where he was going, and for a moment Roxie thought she might get away. But then Helvetia reached shore next, and *she* tackled Roxie, digging her sharp teeth into Roxie's leg.

If a bear bites you on the arm or leg, Lord Thistlebottom had written, *do not panic. Hit him on the snout.*

Roxie brought her fist down hard on Helvetia's nose, and when the bully of all bullies opened her mouth with a howl of pain, Roxie ran up the bank just as Freddy Filch and Smoky Jo were coming ashore.

Roxie may have been the fastest swimmer, but she knew that no matter how fast she ran, Smoky Jo was faster. Now that she had rolled onto Simon's back and hit Helvetia on the nose, they would be like angry bees after her, and spying tall sea grass ahead, Roxie ran for cover.

When chased by a swarm of bees, Lord Thistlebottom had written, *do not panic. Head for a field of tall grass, if possible, and this will impede their progress.*

It impeded the hooligans' progress, all right, but it slowed Roxie's as well. When she reached some woods beyond the sea grass, she headed for a tall tree and began to climb—up, up—until she reached the highest branches. And there she clung, frightened and exhausted, too tired to go on.

The hooligans followed as far as the tree, but no one tried to climb it. They were too worn out and, most of all, they were thirsty. They sank down on the ground and leaned against the trunk, trying to catch their breath.

Finally Helvetia said, "She can't stay up there forever. And when she comes down, we'll get her, all right. We'll fix her wagon!"

"We'll punch out her lights!" growled Simon Surly.

"We'll clear her deck!" panted Freddy Filch.

"We'll clean her plate!" squeaked Smoky Jo.

And then the hooligans lay still.

Up in the treetop Roxie was thirsty too. The salty ocean was still on her tongue, and she tried not to think about the water fountain back at school or the jug of iced tea in her mother's refrigerator.

Down below, the hooligans stretched themselves out in the little bit of sunlight that filtered through the trees, hoping to dry their clothes. No one strayed very far from the others for fear of getting lost. Perhaps they thought that surely—*surely*—someone would come looking for them soon.

Morning became afternoon, however, and the shadows began to lengthen. Night was coming on, and Roxie thought that once the hooligans went to sleep, she could climb down and get away. But then she thought of the night creatures that might be creeping about in the woods, and she decided to stay where she was.

The sky went from gray to purple and from purple to black. Roxie could not see her hand in front of her face. One by one, the hooligans began to snore. Helvetia sounded like a chain saw; Simon sounded like the sea; and a snore that sounded like a pesky mosquito could only belong to Smoky Jo.

Then Roxie heard another noise coming from below. It was not the sea, not the wind, not an animal. It was the soft frightened sob of a boy.

Roxie listened, surprised. She waited, wanting to be sure. And then she whispered down, "Freddy?"

There was no answer. For a long time only the chain saw, the sea, and the mosquito could be heard. Then the sob came again.

"Freddy?" Roxie said. "What's the matter?"

And finally he answered back, "I'm scared."

"Of what?" asked Roxie.

"The dark," sobbed Freddy.

"That's okay," said Roxie. "Sometimes I'm scared a lot too."

But Helvetia had woken now, and it wasn't okay with her. "Scared of the *dark*?" she scoffed. "You'd better quit sniveling, Freddy, or *I'll* give you something to be scared about!"

The woods were quiet after that.

• SNAKE EYES •

When Roxie woke, it was early morning. She had not fallen out of the tree, but she was leaning dangerously off the side of the branch.

Slowly she righted herself and wiggled her neck to get out the kinks. Her mouth felt dry and fuzzy, and she realized that she had not had anything to drink since breakfast the day before.

The hooligans were waking up as well, and all

they could think about, too, was water. They were so thirsty that, for a moment, anyway, they seemed to have forgotten Roxie Warbler up in the tree. But as Helvetia Hagus yawned and stretched, she saw Roxie perched in the upper branches.

Helvetia's jaws closed with a snap. "Hey, Elephant Ears!" she called. "While you're up there, look around and see if there are any ponds or pools or streams or something. Anywhere we could get some water."

Roxie looked, turning herself around on the tree branch so that she could see in all directions. She and the hooligans seemed to be in a woods on the southern end of the island. To the west she saw the long sandy beach where they had come ashore. To the east, where the sun had risen, she saw a jagged shoreline, with waves breaking against the rocks. And to the north she saw tall sea grass waving in the breeze, with more trees beyond. But there was no pond, no pool, no stream.

"I don't see any water," she said.

Her ears, however—her round, pink, sugar-bowl-handle ears—had picked up a new sound that no one else seemed to hear. Once again she turned herself around on the tree branch until she could locate its direction. She saw two men making their way through the sea grass in the middle of the island, and both of them were holding long knives that gleamed in the sun.

They were not dressed like policemen. They were not dressed like hunters. They did not look like soldiers or guards or park rangers, either. They were not wearing safari jackets

with brass buttons, but dirty jeans and torn T-shirts. Roxie's scalp began to tingle, and her hair rose up on her head. Perhaps she had inherited a sixth sense from her uncle when it came to danger, because she knew these men were up to no good.

"Hide!" she hissed to the hooligans below. "I see men with knives, and they're coming this way! Hurry!"

The hooligans had never listened to Roxie before, but there was something about her voice that made them pay attention. Helvetia dived behind a log and covered herself with brush. Simon hid behind a tree. Freddy wedged himself into a hollow stump, and Smoky Jo crawled down a hole and pulled dry leaves in on top of her. Their dull school uniforms helped make them hard to see.

"Don't make a sound!" Roxie told them.

A crow cawed out a warning. A bee made a buzz. A cloud drifted over the blazing sun. And then they all heard it: the *scrunch, scrunch* of footsteps coming closer through the trees, twigs snapping, leaves rustling, feet thudding on the damp earth. Finally Roxie could hear the breathing of the two men as they pushed their way through prickly bushes.

They stopped a few feet away from Roxie's tree to rest. One of the men ran his sleeve across his forehead.

"I tell you, Rat, there's nobody here," he said in a deep voice. "We've searched the whole island."

"And I'm tellin' you I heard somebody cryin' last night," the second man said. He pulled a plug of tobacco from his shirt pocket and bit off a piece. "Maybe a kid."

"Coulda been an old hooty owl or a coyote," said the first man.

"Out here on this island? How could a coyote get all the way out here, I ask you?" said the man named Rat.

"Well, if somebody's here, he won't be going back," said the first man, the larger of the two. "Anybody on this island besides us, I'll slit his throat."

Roxie was trembling so hard, she wondered if she was shaking the tree.

"You're a hard-hearted one, Snake Eyes," said Rat.

"Now, don't you go gettin' soft," Snake Eyes said, looking about him in all directions. "I pulled off the robbery, didn't I? Got us each a million bucks, didn't I? All we have to do is lie low till they stop lookin' for us out this way, and then we'll row down the coast and spend that money in Foot-in-Mouth."

"Can't happen too soon for me," said Rat. "I sure am gettin' tired of fish for dinner."

"And we won't even have that if we don't catch some more today," Snake Eyes told him. "Let's go back to camp and get those fishing lines in the water."

But the smaller man continued to grumble. "Why'd we bother bringing food with us if we're not gonna eat it, Snake Eyes?"

"Because we don't know how long we'll have

to stay here, stupid. What if the weather turns bad and the fish don't bite? What if the rabbits get smart and keep away from our traps? Long as we can make do with what we find on the island, we can save our sausage and cheese for a rainy day," said Snake Eyes. "You hear that old hooty owl again tonight, you wake me and I'll prove it's no kid."

Both men paused again, Rat chewing hard on his tobacco, and then, after a final look around, they tucked their knives in their belts and headed back the way they had come, through the sea grass. Roxie watched as long as she could, but then they disappeared into the trees on the north end of the island.

For almost five minutes nobody moved. Roxie herself felt almost frozen with fright, but finally the brush rustled below and Helvetia's head poked out.

"Psst!" she hissed to Roxie. "Are they gone?"

Roxie nodded. "Yes," she said softly. Her legs were cramped from being in the tree for so long, but if she climbed down, she had not only Helvetia and the hooligans to worry about, but men with knives as well. If ever she wished she had her Uncle Dangerfoot's slender cane, which could, in an instant, become a harpoon, a gun, an umbrella, or a walking stick, depending on the circumstances and the weather, it was now. If ever she wished she were as brave as Lord Thistlebottom, it was this very moment.

All the other hooligans came crawling from their hiding places, with twigs and leaves stuck in their hair.

"*You* heard them, Helvetia!" Smoky Jo squeaked. "They've robbed a bank, and they're hiding out *here*!"

"And they'll slit the throat of anyone they find on the island!" whispered Freddy Filch, his voice shaky.

Helvetia ran her tongue over her dry lips and looked up at Roxie. "Well, Big Ears, you got us into this. You have any ideas? If you don't, and those men come back, we'll make sure you're the first one they catch."

• A SLIMY SANDWICH •

Helvetia's Hooligans stood at the bottom of the tree, their angry eyes on Roxie Warbler.

"I'm *hungry,* too!" said Freddy Filch. "What if nobody comes to rescue us? What if we starve?"

"Yeah," said Smoky Jo. "I didn't have any breakfast yesterday. I need to eat something *now.*" She walked over to the trunk of the tree and sized it up. She looked as though she could eat *Roxie.*

But Roxie was just as hungry and thirsty as they were, and she was getting tired of all their whining. "So eat!" she said from the safety of the tree.

"Eat *what*?" said Simon, glaring at her.

"Grasshoppers, ants, moths, caterpillars . . ."

"Eeuww!" said all the hooligans together.

"Ha!" said Helvetia. "I'd like to see *you* eat something that disgusting."

And right then Roxie knew how she could get down out of the tree without getting punched and pounded. "All right, I will!" she said, and down she came.

The hooligans stared and moved in a little closer.

"There's a big black ant crawling on my shoe," said Freddy, his finger pointing. "You can have it."

"Something better than that," said Roxie.

Simon swooped down and trapped a grasshopper in his hands. His lips curled in a cruel smile. "Eat this!" he said.

"Better than that," said Roxie.

Smoky Jo dug gleefully around in the damp earth and suddenly stood up with a worm draped over her stick. She held it in front of Roxie's face. "Eat *this*!" she said, and her beady eyes gleamed.

"Better than that," said Roxie.

"Ha!" said Helvetia. ""What are you looking for? A hot fudge sundae?"

But Roxie walked on slowly through the trees, the hooligans at her heels. She knew from reading Lord Thistlebottom's book that if she ate something without cooking it, she might get sick. And if she was going to get sick, she had better eat only one thing, something spectacular.

She studied the bushes. She studied the leaves. She kicked at a clump of dirt.

"I've got it!" said Helvetia, capturing a woolly caterpillar and dangling it in front of Roxie's mouth. "Chow down, Big Ears!"

"Better than that," Roxie told her. And then she found what she was looking for. There was a rotting log directly in the path ahead, and already she could see insects hurrying in and out.

Helvetia saw it too and began to smile. "Ah! Breakfast for Roxie Warbler!" she said. The hooligans gathered around.

Roxie knelt down beside the log. She took a stick and began to poke at the rotten part. Bugs fell out. Worms fell out. But Roxie kept digging and poking until she came upon some large white grubs, as thick as her thumb, feasting on the decayed wood.

She reached in and picked up a grub. A wiggly, squirmy, slimy grub. Her stomach began to churn. Her throat felt tight. *When faced with starvation,* Lord Thistlebottom had written, *do not panic. Wrap the insect in something more pleasing and imagine yourself having dinner at Buckingham Palace.*

Roxie knew she could not jump from planes. She could not face a charging rhino or swim through a river of crocodiles, but she could do this.

She wrapped the grub in a dandelion leaf. Then, sitting down on a stump with the hooligans looking on, she opened her mouth.

I am sitting with the queen at Buckingham Palace,

eating a dainty lobster and lettuce sandwich, she told herself.

Crunch. Her teeth came down on the grub, and she bit it in two. It wiggled a little on her tongue. The dandelion leaf gave off a sharp tangy taste. The grub was cool and somewhat slimy, but Roxie chewed twice, then swallowed. *Gulp.*

Roxie put the rest in her mouth. The hooligans' eyes were as big and round as coat buttons. They could not believe that, having taken one nasty bite, she would take another.

"She ate it!" Freddy said to the others.

"Raw!" said Helvetia.

"All of it!" said Simon.

"Live!" said Smoky Jo.

Simon Surly glanced around uneasily. "If we

had to . . . if nobody comes to get us . . . what else can we eat?" he asked.

"No caterpillars with fuzz on them, no bright-colored bugs," said Roxie. "Those could be poisonous. And before you eat a grasshopper, pull off the legs and wings."

"Hey, Big Ears, how do *you* know so much about it?" asked Helvetia.

"Oh, I just read it in a book," Roxie answered.

"*What* book?" asked Simon.

"Lord Thistlebottom's Book of Pitfalls and How to Survive Them," Roxie said.

"Lord Thistlebottom, the famous explorer?" said Simon.

"*You* read his book?" asked Helvetia. And all the hooligans began to laugh.

"She should read a book called *How to Walk*

to School Without Getting Creamed," said Simon.

"She's so scared of us, she spent the night in a tree!" squeaked Smoky Jo.

Freddy was the only one who didn't taunt her.

Roxie looked around at her tormentors and then at the rotten log. "Grub sandwich, anyone?" she asked.

There wasn't any more laughing after that.

• ROXIE'S PLAN •

The hooligans wouldn't eat anything, however, and as morning wore on all anyone could think about was water. Roxie was desperately thirsty too.

"We won't last very long if we don't get water soon," said Helvetia. "Anyone got an idea?" She was looking, of course, at Roxie.

"If those men are hiding out here," Roxie told

the hooligans, "they must have brought some water with them as well as food. And they probably came in a boat. If we can find it, maybe we can get home again."

"Never mind the boat," said Simon Surly, his dry lips sticking together as he talked. "I just want a drink."

"Well, since we don't have any water of our own, we'll just have to borrow some of theirs," said Roxie.

"And who's going to do *that*?" said Helvetia.

"Someone tall and skinny who can hide behind trees," said Roxie. "Someone like Simon."

"Oh, no! Not me!" said Simon Surly.

"Why not?" asked Helvetia.

Simon Surly thought for a moment. "I'm allergic to bark," he said.

"What?" said Helvetia. "One of you is afraid of the dark, and one is allergic to *bark*? What kind of hooligans *are* you, anyway?"

This time Smoky Jo was the only one who laughed.

"Then I guess I'll go myself," said Roxie. And—with the hooligans staring after her—off she went. She could never capture a rogue elephant, she knew, and she might never survive an avalanche, but she could do this.

Her clothes were still damp from the day before. Her shirt clung to her body, her brown and green skirt had lost its pleats. The sweater was filthy from sand and seaweed, and her kneesocks had three holes in one and four in the other. Her shoes seemed to have shrunk on her feet.

It was dark in the woods. It was scary. Roxie moved as if she were stalking deer. *Ten slow steps forward and stop. Wait. Ten slow steps and stop. Wait*—just as Lord Thistlebottom had instructed in his book. She did not know if the men were camped here in the woods at the south end of the island or camped in the trees at the north end. *Ten steps more. Wait. Ten steps more. Wait.*

Finally she reached the sea grass, and peeping out from behind a tree, Roxie saw the two robbers heading off to the east side of the island with some fishing line. When she was quite sure they were out on the rocks, she crept through the sea grass until she finally saw their tent in the trees beyond. Her heart pounded so hard, she was almost afraid the men could hear it.

Step by step, step by step, she pushed her way

through the brush until she came to the tent. She stopped. She listened. Then she stepped just inside, afraid to go any farther.

There were two sleeping bags, a pile of clothes, a couple of pans, sacks, and boxes.

Somewhere in those boxes there must be water, but once inside the tent, there was only one way out. What if the men came back?

Roxie went back out again and moved through the tall sea grass until she could see both men over on the rocks. Then, breathing hard, she slipped back inside the tent and over to the stuff piled in one corner.

She looked through the sacks and stopped to listen for footsteps.

A *swish, swish* sound came from outside. Frantically, she dived for the tent opening. But

the men were still on the rocks, and what she had heard was only the wind blowing the sea grass.

Roxie went back a third time. This time, when she lifted a sack, she saw that the box beneath was filled with plastic bottles of water. Quickly, Roxie took five of the bottles. She stuck one down the waistband of her skirt, tucked one under her left arm, one under her right, and with a bottle in each hand, she crept back out of the tent and started off through the sea grass.

Looking toward the sea, however, she saw only one man on the rocks. Her heart leaped, and she stood frozen where she was. But then the second man's head appeared a little farther on, and their backs were bent over their fishing gear. Roxie moved on, her footsteps in time with her beating heart.

When she was quite sure she could not be seen, she stopped and took the cap off one of the bottles. Slowly, slowly, she drank four long gulps. Then she walked on to where the hooligans were waiting for her. When they saw her coming, they licked their parched lips and grabbed for the bottles, but Roxie held up one hand. "Only four swallows each," she warned them.

"Yeah? Who says?" said Simon, grabbing one for himself.

"I says!" said Helvetia, whacking him on the head. "Four swallows each, just like she said. When it's gone, it's gone."

One by one, each hooligan took a turn with the bottle, the rest watching and counting the number of swallows.

"Five! You took five, Simon!" Smoky Jo said accusingly.

"So what?" said Simon. He handed the bottle back, however. "I'm hungry, I'm tired, and my clothes are still wet."

"Mine too," said Freddy Filch. "I hate this place."

"How long are we going to be here, anyway?" squeaked Smoky Jo in her not-quite-so-mean little mouse voice.

"Someone should be looking for us by now," said Roxie. "The teacher will have missed us in class yesterday, and our parents know we didn't come home from school."

"My parents won't miss me!" said Helvetia, putting the cap back on the bottle. "I'll bet they said, 'Good riddance.'"

"Yeah," said Freddy. "I wouldn't be surprised if my dad didn't even know I was gone."

"Mine either," said Smoky Jo.

Roxie sat down at the end of a log. Her clothes were wet too, and she was hungry, just like the rest of them. But *she* knew for sure that her parents missed her. She knew for sure that someone wanted her back. And that meant she had something the hooligans didn't: the *best* reason to go home.

• BORROWING •

Back in the village of Chin-in-Hand, Roxie figured, families were probably sitting down to simple suppers of cabbage and potatoes. Or beans and franks or biscuits and gravy. She wished she had some of that now. A single biscuit. Half a potato. An onion, even.

"I'm *hungry*!" Smoky Jo complained. "I'm so hungry, I could eat my shirt."

"I'm so hungry, I could eat my sneakers," said Freddy.

"Help yourself," grumbled Helvetia."There're plenty to go around."

"I'll be glad to find some grubs if we have to," Roxie offered.

"Give it one more day," said Helvetia. "I'm not *that* hungry yet."

The four hooligans sat miserably together, some on the log and some on the ground. All held their stomachs to hide the sound of their rumblings. All licked their lips, wanting another drink.

"What if we drink all our water and still nobody comes?" said Simon. "What do we do then?"

"We could make a bucket out of bark and

collect rainwater," Roxie suggested, thinking of the photo in Lord Thistlebottom's book.

"And what if it doesn't rain?" asked Freddy.

Roxie had an answer for that, too. "Then we could tear our shirts into strips and tie them around our ankles. Each morning just after the sun comes up, we'd drag them through the sea grass, and the rags would soak up dew. Then we'd hold them over our mouths and wring them out."

Helvetia's eyes narrowed as she studied Roxie. "What'd you do, Elephant Ears? Memorize the whole book?" she asked.

Roxie could not bring herself to tell the hooligans that she was the niece of the famous Mr. Dangerfoot or that she had sat down to tea on two occasions with the even more famous Lord

Thistlebottom from London. How could a girl be connected to them in any way when she was afraid of someone chasing her on the playground?

So Roxie just said, "I've been around."

Simon Surly turned to Helvetia. "Well, if she's been *around,* why don't you send her to the robbers' tent again to bring back some food this time?"

"I think you should send someone small enough to move through the sea grass, if the men are in the woods, and quick enough to dart into the woods, if the men are in the sea grass," said Roxie. "Somebody little like Smoky Jo."

"Don't look at me!" squeaked the leanest little hooligan of them all. "I . . . I . . . get lost really easy."

"What?" said Helvetia. "One of you is afraid of the dark, one is allergic to bark, and one gets lost really easy? I've sure got me a sorry band of hooligans, I'll say that."

"Then why don't *you* go, Helvetia?" asked Simon.

"Because . . . because I'm the commander, and the commander never leaves her post," said Helvetia.

"Never mind," said Roxie. "I'll go myself."

Strangely, she wasn't quite as frightened as she had been the first time. She had never jumped from a burning building or walked across quicksand, but she could do this. Off she went, and when she reached the sea grass, she got down on her belly. She crawled like a crocodile through the willowy weeds, stopping now and then to listen.

When approaching an adversary through high grass, Lord Thistlebottom had written, *avoid the temptation to raise your head and look around. Stay calm and do not panic.*

Roxie's ears—her wonderful, round, pink, handles-on-a-sugar-bowl ears—picked up the faraway sound of a small plane coming closer, closer, till it flew low over the island. Roxie longed to jump up and wave her arms. To yell and let the pilot see her. But she remembered to keep her head down, and she was glad, for as soon as the plane had gone, she heard men's voices in the trees beyond, and it sounded as though Rat and Snake Eyes were having an argument.

"There's that plane again, Snake Eyes," said Rat. "I'd sure like to know if they've seen us."

"And I'd sure like to know if you're lyin' to me

about that water," came the deep voice of Snake Eyes. "I count twenty-one bottles, and there should be twenty-six! We brought two cases of water with us, Rat, and we need every drop we can get. Now where are those other five bottles?"

"Well, *you* tell *me*! How do I know *you* ain't hidin' a bottle every day or two in case we run out? How do I know you ain't gettin' ready to take all the money yourself as well as the food and water and leave me stranded out here?"

"You're talkin' nonsense," said Snake Eyes. "All I'm sayin' is, if you got five bottles stashed away someplace, then I get five bottles to tuck away for myself."

"I tell you I didn't take no five bottles!" said Rat, his voice rising.

"Yeah? Says you."

"That's right. Says me." There was quiet for a while.

Finally Snake Eyes said, "You check that rabbit trap yet?"

"Goin' off to do it now," said Rat. "What about the fishnet we rigged up yesterday?"

"I'll tend to that," said Snake Eyes.

Roxie lay as still as a stick in the sea grass. She heard one man go off one way, one man go off the other.

But now she had to look out in two directions, east and west. If she turned her head one way to follow one of the men, she was turning her back on the other. When their footsteps and grunts and coughs had died away completely, she slowly . . . slowly . . . raised her head. She had only a minute or so, she knew, for she suspected that each man was going to spy on the other.

Roxie crawled on her hands and knees till she reached the end of the sea grass. Then she continued to crawl until she got to the tent.

Quickly! Quickly! Roxie peeked in one sack. Then another. No food there. But in a burlap bag on one side of the tent she found tins of tuna and sardines, cans of beef stew and spaghetti and beans. She had no can opener, however, so she settled for a large smoked sausage and a round of cheese.

Stuffing them both under her shirt and into the waistband of her skirt, Roxie began her crawl once more through the sea grass. She had not gotten thirty feet from the tent when she heard the men coming back. She flattened herself on the ground, knowing that if she continued to crawl, they might see the way the sea grass parted to let her pass. She felt as though her heart would explode as it thumped against the earth beneath her.

"Anything in your trap?" Snake Eyes called to Rat.

"Somethin' took the dang bait, but I didn't catch it," said Rat. "Fishing line bring anything?"

"Nuthin' worth cooking up. By the time you take the bones out of it, it'd be just fins and tail," grumbled Snake Eyes.

Their voices seemed so close to her now that Roxie was sure they must be looking down on her at that very moment. She closed her eyes in terror. The silence went on for another minute or two, and then she could tell by the mens' voices that they had gone back inside the tent.

Roxie edged forward and stopped. Two feet more, and stopped. Two feet more . . . When she reached the trees at last and the men hadn't followed, she was so relieved that she allowed herself one big bite each of cheese and sausage. Nothing had ever tasted so good. There would be no grub sandwich today, anyway.

Just as before, when she got back, the hooligans rushed to meet her, and this time Smoky Jo tried to grab the food out of her hands.

"Where are your manners?" Roxie said, jerking the food away again. "You can eat one bite of each. We've got to make it last."

"*You* already had a bite," complained Simon.

"And so could you if *you* had been the one to fetch it," said Helvetia. "Shut up and eat your sausage."

When each of the hooligans had taken a bite, Helvetia wrapped the rest up in her sweater. They sat morosely on the log, wishing they could have more.

"This time the men will *know* someone was in their tent," Roxie warned them. "They're bound to come looking again."

"What are we going to do?" asked Freddy. "Where can we hide?"

Roxie tried to think what her uncle would tell her to do. As far as she could remember, there was no chapter in Lord Thistlebottom's book about where to hide from robbers on an island. But she remembered his advice on what to do when lost in the mountains: *Do not panic. Use a stick to dig a trench in the snow. Get in it and cover yourself with leaves and branches.*

Digging in dirt was a lot harder than digging in snow, she knew, but the soil was loose and sandy, and there was nowhere else to hide. If they went down to the beach, the men might see them. If they went to the rocks, the men could corner them there.

"Let's dig a long trench we can sleep in tonight," Roxie suggested. "We'll cover ourselves with leaves and branches, and one of us will be the lookout."

Dig they did. Some of them used their hands, the others used sticks. After an hour or so they had carved out a trench just long enough and wide enough for all of them to lie in together. They spread out the pile of dirt they had unearthed and covered it with leaves so there would be no sign of their digging. Then they dragged over some branches to cover themselves.

"Who will be the lookout?" asked Roxie, but before the question was out of her mouth, Helvetia and her hooligans had already crawled down inside the trench and were squeezed together all in a row.

"Never mind," said Roxie. "I guess I'll do it myself." She covered the four with thick fir branches, then stretched out on the log and studied the stars. For once she was glad that her ears stuck far out from her head, because she was able to hear the faintest birdcall, the slightest puff of wind, the merest snap of a twig. And so she lay, ears tuned to the night.

• THE RABBIT NOISE •

It was a bit lonely there on the log while the hooligans slept, Roxie decided. The night was dark, and she was still very hungry.

She was more hungry when she had nothing else to do but lie on a log and think about food. A nice piece of fried chicken, perhaps. A chewy cookie with chocolate chunks. A hot bowl of her mother's tomato soup with a thick slice of buttered bread . . .

She wondered what her parents were doing right then. They must be sick with worry, she imagined. The people of Chin-in-Hand would wonder how five schoolchildren could just disappear in a single day.

Roxie studied the little piece of sky that she could see through the leaves. There was only a sliver of moon, but the stars were bright, and as the earth moved and one star after another disappeared from view, Roxie reminded herself that she must not fall asleep.

It was when she noticed that the black of the sky had turned gray and the gray was turning pink that she heard the noise—a far-off scrunching of twigs and leaves. *Footsteps!*

She rolled off the log and tumbled over to the trench. "Someone's coming!" she whispered.

"Don't move. Don't sneeze. Don't make a sound." Then she hid herself in a thicket.

In a few minutes Roxie could hear the voices of Rat and Snake Eyes but could barely see them in the early dawn. They stopped not ten feet from where the hooligans were lying, and Snake Eyes said, "See, Rat? There's no one else on the island!"

"Then if anyone's eatin' our food and drinkin' our water, it's you," said Rat. "I don't know why you don't own up to it 'stead of sayin' it's *me* who's eatin' more than his share."

"Now, *you* listen," said Snake Eyes. "I divided up that food fair and square. A can for you, a can for me. A bag for you, a bag for me. Now we got some missing, same as the water, and I think it's you tuckin' some of it away so if we run out, it'll be me who goes with the empty stomach. I'm sorry I ever let you in on this."

"Well, don't think I'm not sorry already!" said Rat. "Livin' out here like savages, gettin' eaten up by 'skeeters, runnin' for cover every time a plane comes over . . ."

And right at that moment there it was again—the drone of a plane in the distance, growing louder all the time. It flew low over the island just as before, then it went on.

Rat and Snake Eyes waited a minute to see if the plane would come back. When it didn't, they moved on through the brush, coming so close to the trench that Roxie sucked in her breath, afraid that one of them might step through the branches and fall in.

She heard Snake Eyes say, "Well, it's not

going to do no good to fight. When we get off this island, we can each have us a house with a dozen rooms in it, and we'll never have to look at each other again."

"That's okay with me," said Rat. "Have to say I'm gettin' right sick of seein' your face each morning, last thing I look at before I sleep at night."

Grumpily, they went on, and Roxie gave a long, relieved sigh. She crawled over to the trench when she was sure they were gone and told the hooligans they could come out.

Stiff and frightened, Helvetia and Simon and Freddy and Smoky Jo emerged from the hole and sat on the log, arms wrapped around themselves to ward off the chill.

"You almost had those robbers down there in

the trench with you," said Roxie. "They were *this* close to stepping on you!" and she showed them with her hands.

"It's awful down there," said Smoky Jo. "A mouse even crawled in during the night."

"I thought someone would come looking for us by now," said Freddy in a small voice.

"I'm hungry and thirsty both," said Simon.

There was quiet in the little gathering. And then Helvetia asked, "What do you think we should do, Roxie?"

It was the first time Helvetia Hagus had called Roxie by her real name. The first time she had not said something about Roxie's ears.

"Well," said Roxie, "a plane came by yesterday and a plane came by today. A search plane

looking for us, I'll bet. But it won't know we're here unless we give it a sign."

And what kind of a sign would *that* be?" growled Simon. "Where are we going to get a billboard ten feet high?"

"We're going to make a distress signal on the beach out of rocks," said Roxie. And she recited the second paragraph on page sixty of *Lord Thistlebottom's Book of Pitfalls and How to Survive Them:* "'To attract the attention of rescuers, the unlucky traveler should make a large triangle of any available material and place in a location that can be easily seen from a distance. Do not panic.'"

"How can we make a triangle out of rocks?" asked Smoky Jo. "The rocks are on one side of the island. The beach is on the other."

"We'll form a rock brigade," said Roxie.

"Simon will go to the cliff and hand rocks to Helvetia. Helvetia will carry them through the sea grass to Freddy. Freddy will bring them down to me on the beach, and I'll make a triangle on the sand."

"And what will *I* do?" squeaked Smoky Jo.

"You'll be the lookout," said Roxie. "You need to hide up by the robbers' camp, and if either of them leaves the tent, you give the call."

"What's the call?" asked Smoky Jo. "The men will hear!"

"They'll hear, but they won't know what it is," said Roxie. "Everybody lick the back of your hand."

"What?" said Helvetia.

"Make it good and wet," said Roxie. "Spit on it if you have to."

The hooligans stared at her. Roxie demonstrated on her own hand, and the hooligans giggled as they slopped and slathered their skin.

"Now," said Roxie, remembering what she had learned from Uncle Dangerfoot, "give that hand a long, slow kiss, and it will sound like a squalling rabbit." She put her mouth to the back of her hand and kissed, and the sucking, smacking sound was indeed one that Helvetia's Hooligans had never heard before.

"Why would anyone want to sound like a squalling rabbit?" asked Freddy.

"To attract other animals that might like a nice fat rabbit for dinner," said Roxie. "A fox, maybe. And then the hunter kills the fox."

In a matter of seconds all the hooligans were making the squalling rabbit noise, and Roxie remembered the times she would lie in bed on a Saturday morning, making those wild and crazy noises until her mother would come to the door of her room and say, "Roxie, dear, please! The neighbors will think you are ill."

At last Roxie held up her hand to stop the commotion before it got so loud that the men might hear. The hooligans paid attention.

"Now," Roxie continued, "if you hear Smoky Jo make the rabbit noise, pass it on to the next person. That will mean the men are leaving their tent and you have to hide."

So Simon Surly set off for the rocky cliffs.

Helvetia set off for the sea grass. Freddy hid himself on the hill above the beach, and Roxie helped Smoky Jo find a hiding place near the robbers' tent. Then she went down to the beach alone.

• THE ROCK BRIGADE •

For a long time Roxie waited and listened. Listened and waited. Then she saw Freddy coming toward her with a big rock in his hands. Roxie took it from him and carried it down to the watermark in the sand. While she waited for another rock, she looked about for any she might find there herself, and slowly—as another rock arrived and then the next—a triangle, the international sign of distress, Lord Thistlebottom had written, began to form on the sand.

For an hour Roxie worked without stopping. Freddy hauled rocks without complaint. It was a large triangle—one that Roxie knew could be seen from the air. She had two sides done and half of the third when, from far off, she heard the rabbit cry.

Roxie straightened up and looked around. She heard another rabbit cry, this one coming from the other side of the island, and shortly after that a third cry from the sea grass.

But which way were the robbers coming? Roxie wondered, and where should she hide? Crouching low, she scrambled up the grassy bank.

Then she heard the men's voices.

"What the dad-gum is it?" Rat called to Snake Eyes. "Some kind of animal, but I'll be danged if I know what it is."

"Could be some kind of critter we've never seen before," Snake Eyes called back. "Like some of those creatures down in Australia or something."

"*Where* the heck is it?" said Rat. "Sounds like there's more than one. Could be all over the place."

"Might make a tasty dinner, if we could catch one," said Snake Eyes.

The small plane they had heard that morning was coming back again, and this time Roxie heard Rat say, "I think they're after us, Snake Eyes. I think they know where we're hidin' out."

"*I'm* thinkin' we ought to clear out, head

down the coast," said Snake Eyes. "Those deputies like to come in the early morning and surprise you. I'm bettin' they'll try to come here tomorrow before we're awake. Well, we'll just surprise them. Clear out and be gone before they get here."

Roxie made it back to the woods on the south end of the island, and twenty minutes later all five children had gathered and were eating the last of the sausage and cheese and laughing at the way they had confused the two robbers.

They heard the small plane again, but just as before, it flew over the island and went on.

"Maybe the next time we hear it coming, we should all run down to the beach and take our chances," said Roxie, when an hour had gone by and the plane hadn't returned. "Maybe we should stand down there waving our arms and yelling."

"Even if the pilot saw us, though, there's no place for him to land," said Simon.

"And even if he could land, there would still be time for Snake Eyes to catch us and slit our throats," added Smoky Jo. But even that wasn't enough to stop the smile that was spreading across her face. "You should have seen old Snake Eyes when he got up to leave his tent and I made that rabbit noise!" she said.

They all began to smile.

"He almost fell over, it surprised him so," she went on. "He couldn't see me because I was in a thicket, but he was coming my way, and then Freddy, *he* gave the rabbit sound, and Snake Eyes started over there. Then Helvetia gave the cry from the sea grass, and Simon had a turn, and those robbers didn't know which way was up."

Simon guffawed and made the rabbit noise again just for fun. Then Helvetia made the rabbit sound, and soon all five children—Roxie included—were at it again.

"I can't wait to try it on Miss Crumbly when she's at the blackboard," said Simon.

"Try it on the playground!" said Helvetia. "We could get all the kids doing it."

Everyone laughed then. Helvetia brayed, Simon howled, Freddy cawed, and Smoky Jo squeaked like a mouse. And suddenly, as quickly as it had started, the laughter stopped, and all five children looked up to find themselves staring into the gleaming eyes of Rat and Snake Eyes.

Do not panic.

Roxie repeated the words in her head even as her feet pounded on the forest floor. Five children scattered in five different directions, and the roar of the men sounded like wild animals behind them.

As Roxie ran she realized that if she were to hear a squeal or a squall now, she would not know if it was the rabbit noise she had learned from Uncle Dangerfoot or one of the hooligans being caught. She was surprised to find that she cared.

She decided to head for the beach. At least if the robbers cornered her there, she could swim out to sea and take her chances with a shark. Better a shark than Snake Eyes and his knife. He would surely kill them all, for he wouldn't want any children, if rescued, telling the police where the robbers had been hiding.

And there he came, close behind her. A shoe came off as Roxie ran across the sand. *If a bull charges,* Lord Thistlebottom had written, *do not panic. Throw away an article of clothing and the bull will probably head for that.*

Roxie took off her sweater and threw it right in Snake Eyes's face. It slowed him for a moment but did not stop him, and his hand almost grabbed her as he lunged forward again.

Then Roxie heard it. Her magnificent, wonderful, round, pink, sugar-bowl-handle ears caught the far-off sound of an engine. The small plane was coming back!

But it was not a plane. Not a boat. Coming

down out of the sky, like a huge bird, was a helicopter, and as Roxie ran out into the water to escape the robber, she saw a rope ladder tumble out of the helicopter till it hung five feet above the surf. And then . . . *then* . . . out of the helicopter and down the ladder came her uncle.

• OUT OF THE SKY •

Up in the sea grass the hooligans saw Uncle Dangerfoot too and began to cheer.

Rat, who had caught Simon Surly by the throat, let go when he saw the helicopter and took off running through the woods.

Down on the sand Snake Eyes skidded to a stop at the water's edge and stared open-mouthed at the man in the jungle hat and the safari jacket, climbing down a rope ladder toward the sea.

When Uncle Dangerfoot reached the bottom rung of the ladder, he reached down and grabbed Roxie's hand.

Up, up she climbed until she reached the opening in the belly of the helicopter. And there, helping to pull her in, was Norman, from Public School Number Thirty-Seven.

"Norman!" she cried.

"Roxie!" he said. "The hooligans took my glasses, and I couldn't see what was happening to you."

But the biggest surprise was yet to come, for when the pilot turned around to welcome her aboard, Roxie saw that it was Lord Thistlebottom himself, all the way from London.

"When your mother told me that you were missing," Uncle Dangerfoot explained, climbing back into the helicopter, "I called Lord Thistlebottom, and in less than an hour he was on his way."

"And then," said Lord Thistlebottom, "your friend Norman here—a fine lad, indeed—remembered a terrible noise about the time you disappeared from the playground."

"So we put two and two together . . . ," said Roxie's uncle.

"Four, as it were . . . ," said Lord Thistlebottom.

"And when the search plane spotted the triangle made of rocks . . . ," said Uncle Dangerfoot.

". . . the pilot radioed back to us, and we

knew it had to be someone who had read my book," Lord Thistlebottom finished. "So out we came in this helicopter, and we brought Norman along. He said you had disappeared in the company of hooligans."

The helicopter was descending now over the beach, and sand flew every which way.

"Hooligans, yes, but right now they're in danger!" said Roxie. "There are two bank robbers hiding out here, Uncle Dangerfoot, and they said they would slit the throat of anyone they found on the island!"

"By Jove, this is a jolly adventure!" cried Lord Thistlebottom, adjusting his cravat, and Uncle Dangerfoot reached for his slender cane, which could, in an instant, become a harpoon, a gun, an umbrella, or a walking stick, depending on the circumstances and the weather.

"We'll just see about that, won't we, Lord Thistlebottom?" he said.

"We'll give them a run for their money—or should I say, the bank's money?" cried Lord Thistlebottom, and he turned to his instruments and radioed the police.

"Now, where are the hooligans Norman was telling us about?" asked Uncle Dangerfoot, opening the door of the helicopter and stepping out onto the sand.

"There they are! Here they come!" said Roxie as Helvetia and Simon and Freddy and Smoky Jo, their eyes wide with wonder, dashed across the beach.

One after the other, they climbed into the helicopter as Uncle Dangerfoot counted them off with a light whack on their bottoms with his cane.

"What about *them*?" Helvetia said, pointing to Rat and Snake Eyes, who had pulled a motorboat out of its hiding place and were trying to make their escape.

"A patrol boat is on its way," said Lord Thistlebottom, "and those thieves think they can outrace it. We'll see about that."

The helicopter flew on ahead of the speeding boat and began to come closer and closer to the water. The wind it created stirred up waves, and the boat tossed this way and that.

Desperately, the robbers turned their boat around and went tearing off in the direction they had come, only to see the patrol boat coming toward them. With the police ahead of them, the helicopter behind, land on one side of them, and the wide ocean on the other, Rat and Snake Eyes jumped overboard and tried to swim away, but the jig was up, and the officers pulled them into the police boat. Roxie said she was sure that if the policemen searched the island, they would find the bank's money hidden somewhere.

"A fine day! Fine, indeed!" said Uncle Dangerfoot, beaming proudly at his niece.

"A jolly good adventure, that!" Lord Thistlebottom added with a chuckle. "Jolly good show, Roxie Warbler."

Back over the ocean they went, skimming over waves and fishing boats and then, at last, over land. Villages and towns sped by below, and

Roxie held her breath for fear the helicopter would touch the treetops. Over Hasty Pudding they flew, over Hamburger-on-Bun. Then Swiss-on-Rye, till at last she recognized the church steeple of Chin-in-Hand, and the helicopter began to descend.

There was Public School Number Thirty-Seven, there was the playground, and there was the bright blue Dumpster waiting for its next load to take to the sea. And finally there they were, getting a grand welcome from Miss Crumbly and all the other children, cheering and waving a banner that said WELCOME BACK.

The hooligans stared, for no one had ever welcomed them anywhere. They could not believe that the gingersnaps and lemonade were really for them, and even though they had not

WELCOME BACK
Welcome back

had a decent meal in three days, they offered the platter first to Roxie and Norman before they took any for themselves.

But the best welcome was the one Roxie got when she returned home.

"There she is!" her mother cried when Roxie came up the walk. Her parents hugged her so hard, she could scarcely breathe.

That evening Roxie Warbler, freshly bathed and combed and wearing her patent-leather shoes and her best blue dress, sat with her feet on a footstool in the family parlor, a teacup in one hand, a crumpet in the other, and told Uncle Dangerfoot and Lord Thistlebottom, as well as her parents, all that had happened since she had been dumped in the sea.

Uncle Dangerfoot listened intently, occasionally tapping his long slender cane on the floor. Lord Thistlebottom reached for another crumpet and smiled with delight as Roxie told of the trench, the rock brigade, and the rabbit noises she had learned from his book. Mrs. Warbler sat to one side holding a plate of crumpets, should Roxie want more, and her dad sat on the other side, ready to go for the sugar if Roxie wanted another lump.

"Oh, it was harrowing, let me tell you," said the girl with the remarkable, magnificent, wonderful, round, pink, sugar-bowl-handle ears. "It was uncharted territory there on the island, and our mouths had long since gone dry, but you will be glad to know, Uncle Dangerfoot, that I remembered all you had taught me."

And seated across the room was the little

band of hooligans, all with teacups balanced on their laps, listening politely. They were known from then on as Roxie's Warblers, for they had only good things to say about her—Roxie, the girl who did not panic, not one little bit.